A BOOK

By Shuna Le Moine

Table of Contents

The Black Dog by the Tree

Billy Bradshaw bought A Book,
he wrote his name inside.
He hid it on the topmost shelf,
then went out for a ride.
He bounced along a bumpy lane,
turned left, then up a hill.
He'd planned to meet his friend at three,
a pretty girl called Jill.

Jilly Jones had bought A Book
and put her name inside.
She'd popped it in her shoulder-bag
then gone off for a ride.
She'd cycled out along the path,
to meet her friend at three.
It really wasn't very far
to that hilltop with the tree.

Billy Bradshaw got there first,
laid his bike down on the ground.
He sat amidst the buttercups
and waited to be found.
When Jill arrived, she smiled, and said
"I've brought A Book to read.
I've got it in my shoulder-bag,
with some other things we'll need.
A thermos flask, some cups of course,
and biscuits for our tea.
I hope you brought your glasses Bill
so you can read to me?"

He smiled and said "Of course I have.
Which story should it be?"
She looked and then decided on
"The Black Dog by the Tree"
She lay down in the buttercups.
She closed her eyes and sighed.
Then turned her imagination key
in a secret door inside.
Billy Bradshaw cleared his throat
and he began to read.
But as he read the words, he thought,
this story's strange indeed!
For it told of Bill, who'd bought A Book
and put his name inside,
then put it on a topmost shelf
and gone off for a ride!

But his naughty sister Mary
had watched him hide his book,
and used their bunk-bed ladder
to climb up and take a look!

The book was full of stories,
words Mary couldn't read.
But the words turned into pictures
so there really was no need.
And the words were magic pictures
which only she could see.
A black dog barked and spoke to her,
invited her to join him.
She took his paw, he pulled, she jumped
and landed right beside him.
As Billy read these words aloud
he grew a little wary.
And when he turned the page
he gasped, for there *was* sister Mary.
And she was looking back at him,
holding a black dog's paw.
Embarrassed to be seen by him,
aware of what he saw.
So Mary smiled and waved to him,
not quite sure what to say.
And the words on the page all followed her
as she turned and ran away.
Now Billy had no words to read.
Blank pages, nothing more.

?

So he put the book down on the ground
and was surprised at what he saw.
For there *was* a black dog by the tree,
wagging his tail, not scary,

And running fast towards them
was his little sister Mary!
"Oh Bill", she laughed,
"I love the book I think you tried to hide.
I took it down to look at
when you went off for your ride.
This lovely dog was trapped in there,
he's so happy to be free.
I really hope you let us come
and join you for some tea?"

The black dog sat and waited,
  as Bill made up his mind...
Was he real or just created?
What else would Mary find?
Was it *really* sister Mary?
Or another child just like?
But it must be, 'cos she knew him
and she knew about his bike...
So, he beckoned them to join him,
'midst the buttercups on the hill.
And they came to share the picnic
  brought by his best friend Jill.
As Jill, it seemed, was fast asleep,
  they let her snooze a while.
'Till the black dog licked her on the nose,
  and she woke up with a smile.

Unexpected Picnic Guests

Jilly Jones woke with a smile -
Something wet had touched her nose!
Then she saw it was the black dog from the book!
She frowned and stroked its head.
She'd heard all Bill had read,
stared at Mary and gave Bill a puzzled look.

"Oh, I thought you'd met before"
said Bill, a bit surprised.
"Mary, may I introduce - My dear chum Jill.
We often come up here for a story and some tea.
It's so peaceful by this tree upon the hill"

Jill said "Pleased to meet you"
(Though indeed she really wasn't
as Mary had disturbed her picnic bliss.
And the black dog, though not big,
seemed to take up half the rug
and she wasn't sure at all she wanted this!)

"Bet you want to know what it's like inside the book?"
Asked Mary, clearly brimming full of joy.
And Jill said "Yes of course."
but that wasn't strictly true
as she'd rather be alone with her boy.

Bill stared hard at Mary, still checking 'she' was 'she',
and decided that the story had come true.
Of course, he was intrigued,
wondered how on earth she'd got there.
But no one seemed to have a single clue.

"Give me the book." said Jill,
"I really want to see it.
To check if all the words *have* disappeared."
Mary laughed and showed her
all the words piled up behind her!
And Jill said "Mary,
that's not funny, it's just weird!"

"It *is* weird inside." said Mary,
and took herself a biscuit.
Jill sighed aloud and grabbed the packet back.
Bill said "Let's have tea, it'll make us all feel better."
The dog agreed, his swishy tail went thwack.

So, Bill poured out the tea.
They had to share the cups.
Of course, the black dog, he was happy to be last.
And Bill asked sister Mary
to show him what had happened.
But she simply couldn't reenact the past.
"So you're both here to stay?"
Jill addressed the black dog

And he nodded and said,
"Hope that you don't mind?"
And Jill asked if she had a choice,
and at first she looked annoyed.
Then felt compassion and decided to be kind.
"So now we have a dog." said Bill and he was smiling.
"And a lovely dog at that." noted Jill.
"And a special dog who talks."
added little sister Mary.
Then they packed their things
and walked back down the hill.

When no one else was looking,
Mary checked behind her,
just in case the words still followed in her wake.
And indeed there they were
and many more had joined them.
They formed a long and bendy shape
just like a snake.
And as more words are spoken
then they all join the others.
They only stop when this story truly ends.
But I think it's time to sleep now.
So close your eyes, breathe calmly
And know that Jill, the dog
and Mary are now friends.

Mary Meets the Blue Boy

Dear young Mary Bradshaw met a dog inside a book.
Though her brother'd put it out of reach,
she'd climbed up to take a look,
when she knew he wouldn't see her,
when he'd gone off on a ride.
And Mary was delighted
to find a dog inside.

The dog was called Anubis.
He was happy as could be,
because his new friend Mary
had somehow set him free.
He'd been inside the book a while,
and before that, inside the head
of an author who'd imagined him
when half asleep in bed.
Anubis was as black as tar,
his tail was long and swishy.
He could talk and smile and understand,
though his breath was slightly fishy.
He was magic too, now he was free
so, all was so exciting.
Now he could do just what he chose,
not rely on the author's writing.
When Mary asked who else was there,
living inside the book.
Anubis said to look out for
The Pirate and The Cook.
He told her of
The Damselfly with the Iridescent wings,
and the haunted church beside the stream
where the Happy Ghost Choir sings.

And he told her of the Boy in Blue
who though looks sweet and nice,
is really, best avoided
for he has a heart of ice.
The Boy in Blue says hurtful things
and he simply doesn't care
if he hurts you, or he tricks you,
he's just horrid and unfair.
"So, you simply must beware of him."
Anubis said to Mary.
"Of the Boy in Blue it's best to know
he's more goblin than he's fairy.
Do NOT *believe* his stories,
that's his *power* to make them true.
Best not follow in his footsteps
you could end up in the poo!"
Mary was a bit surprised
to hear these words of warning.
She'd imagined that the black dog's world
would be fun and not alarming!
The Boy in Blue, oh dear, she thought,
don't want to meet HIM now.

And she wore the black dog's caution
in a furrow on her brow.
The black dog smiled and wagged his tail.
Invited her to follow:
"You must meet Sobek crocodile,
he lives down by the hollow -
He's really such a lovely smile,
shows off his pointy teeth.
And he loves to roll onto his back
so you can stroke his underneath."
"But won't he bite me?" queried Mary,
"with his many pointy teeth?
I've heard its cold and slimy
that yellow underneath."
"Oh, don't worry little Mary."
The black dog he replied.
"He won't bite you, 'cos he's happy,
even though he is cross-eyed.
He's forever searching chances
to show off his loving side -
Such as saving drowning people
or taking ducklings for a ride."

It was at that very moment
that the Boy in Blue appeared.
And his smile surprised our Mary
for at once she felt endeared.
As indeed he was most charming,
took her hand and bowed his head.
And she found instead of fearing
she felt warmly fond instead.
The Boy in Blue held firm her hand
and motioned her to follow,
to "come and see the crocodile
who lives down by the hollow."

"Oh, you mean the dearest Sobek?"
Asked Mary, full of cheer.
The Boy said "Yes, that is his name,
but he's creature you must **fear!**"
"But I thought that he was full of love
and took ducklings for a ride?"
"Pah!" the Boy in Blue laughed back,
"He has no *loving* side!
He's really very vicious,
he has signets for his tea,
and the ducklings that he carries,
they'll get eaten too, you'll see."
"Oh" said Mary, now confused,
recalling the black dog's warning.
Though Anubis he had disappeared
and didn't answer to her calling...
The Blue Boy held her hands in his,
gazed into her dark brown eyes.
He asked her if she trusted him.
She said "Yes" to her surprise.
And he led her to the hollow
where Sobek gnashed his pointy teeth.
And she saw the slimy belly
of the cruel croc's underneath.

The crocodile he snapped and splashed
and whacked his tail in rage.
What a tasty morsel Mary was.
What a very *tender* age.
He looked at little Mary and he
licked his lips with joy.
Little Mary was so frightened
she clung tight to the Blue Boy.

The Blue Boy laughed and taunted her.
Now his eyes looked so much colder.
And Mary realised that she'd believed
the version he had told her -
That Sobek **was** a danger
and ate cygnets for his tea.
For *believing*, she had made it real.
She had *chosen* what would be.
Mary knew that she must change her mind,
Sobek lived inside a story,
where a terrifying crocodile
could be filled with love and glory -
If that is what the author wrote.
If that is how she saw him.
Then that is how this croc could be
in the story book he lived in.
So Mary focussed her attention,
believing Sobek to be kind.
Letting go the Blue Boy's hand
she was free to change her mind.
And Anubis reappeared at once.
He woofed and wagged and smiled.
And lesson 1 was learned just then
by a somewhat wiser child.

Then Mary, she just turned the page
and the Blue Boy was no more.
And Anubis he was walking
towards an open door.
And through the door was brother Billy
in a buttercuppy lea,
reading to his best friend Jilly
who had brought a picnic tea.

The Pirate and the Cook

Young Alex Jones, he wanted an adventure,
life was boring.
All he knew was where he lived,
his Gran's and school.
He felt stranded, like a boat
forever tied to its mooring.
Or an off-road car that hadn't any fuel.
Alex longed to be somewhere
no one knew his name.
Somewhere far away where buses didn't run.
For him, it seemed, that every day was just the same:
home and school, home and school
and not much fun.
Jilly Jones, his twin,
had a better time than he.
To Alex, Jilly's life was so much more exciting.
She would go off on her bike
and have picnics in the lea,
leaving Alex stuck at home to practice writing.

So, one morning, very early,
he dreamt he had a plan
(as he lay in bed, and just before he woke)
And in this clearest dream,
he would stow aboard a ship.
No more a kid but some kind of rugged bloke.
And the bloke he dreamt he was
had an eye patch, and a glint
in the other eye which saw as well as two.
And he wore a scarf about his head,
said "Aaaarh" and had a limp.
He was 'Pirate Alex' with a cutlass to be true.

He dodged about the docks
and he waited for a ship
which would sail to foreign lands he could explore.
But the kind of ship that he'd expected,
with a figurehead and sails
It seemed they sadly were not making anymore.

So he jumped aboard a liner.
It was huge, and so much finer
than a sailing ship with flags along a line.
And he hid inside the loo,
which wasn't hard to do.
And he stayed there
for what seemed quite some time.

And as the boat set sail,
Alex 'pirate' planned his actions.
He'd take a hostage and then rob the lot of gold!
But all who were aboard
were mathematicians learning fractions,
and a school of cooks, some young but mostly old.
So Pirate Alex, he decided, he'd best go incognito.
He would mingle with the cooks to not stand out.
He'd use his pirate's head-scarf
as a jolly kind of apron.
His cutlass would be handy too no doubt.
He joined in all their lessons
and found it was quite fun
to be learning stuff with such a jolly crowd.
He made new friends and pretty soon
forgot he was a pirate.
And all that he was learning made him proud.
After just a week of cooking (in his dream),
Alex Jones was looking slightly fatter
in the face and smiling more.
He could cook a fish 'Bonne Femme',
make superb Tarte Tartin.
Knew the French word for an oven was a 'four'.

In fact, Alex was so keen,
he was more than often seen
stooping down to watch his biscuits as they tanned.
His cakes rose like the sun,
he was having so much fun.
Though of course this was nothing like he'd planned.
Then the ship's alarm rang out,
and all the cooks and crew ran out,
forming rather wobbly lines, rehearsing drill.
As the register was read
each one 'Yes'd as their name said:
Tom Jones, "Yes", Jane Brown "Yes,
Zack Hill...
When all the names were called
'cept that of Alex Jones,
the teacher turned to him,
confused and frowning.
Alex stared down at his shoes,
said there must be some mistake.
He must hurry back to
check his crumble browning.

"But Mr Alex Jones, why aren't you on our list?"
All the others, in their wobbly lines, they stared.
Alex Pirate went bright red -
He'd been rumbled, truth be said.
But in his dream, he was of course prepared.
He drew his cutlass out
and he jumped upon a raft.
All the others ran for shelter,
they were fearful.

But the teacher was a cook
and he clearly wasn't daft,
in fact, a swordsman too and really rather artful.
A swordfight then began,
with ferocious clash and clang.
There were sparks, there were "Oooo"s
and there was gurning.

Then cook teacher checked his watch,
and said he must be off,
elsewise all of their lasagnes would be burning.
And Alex said "Oh no, I must come along as well,
to save the crumble and to check up on my bread!"
So they hurried back inside, to finish off their tasks
as there was a class of mathematicians to be fed.

When everyone had eaten
and each had made a judgement,
giving marks out of a hundred for the dishes.
The crumble came out top,
but the bread it was a flop.
So they threw it overboard for all the fishes.

Then teacher smiled at Alex
and he slapped him on the back.
Alex turned around and both began to laugh.
As they did so he could hear his mother's voice say.
"Wake up dear, it's Wednesday Alex,
time to have your bath."

WEDNESDAY
06:30

Mary's story:
The Damselfly with
the Iridescent Wings

One sunny summer's morning,
when the sky was clear and cool.
We were walking through the woods,
down to the stream.
I breathed the fragrant meadowsweet-heads,
bent down with the dew,
and counted all the different shapes of green.
The nettles, they were tall, and had fallen in my path,
so, I bashed them with my stick to clear the way.
The brambles too, it seemed,
had grown much longer overnight,
so I pushed them back and tried to make them stay.
As we neared the little stream
with the bridge we both knew well,
Anubis ran ahead to have a drink.
I heard him splish and splash,
as he paddled and he dunked,
gulping mouthfuls of cool water tinged with mint

Just as we approached,
I'd watched a creature come to rest
on a slender stem I'd reed and close its wings
It was an iridescent blue
and shone so brightly in the sun.
Like a jewel or some other precious thing.
And the creature turned to me,
as it saw that I was watching,
and asked me if I knew what was the time?
I was, of course, perplexed
it had asked me such a question.
But I checked my watch and said
"It's nearly nine."
As no one else was there,
'cept me and dear Anubis,
I sat down and I waited, just in case...
Did it have something to tell me,
or something else to ask me?
As I waited, I retied my loose boot lace.
"Perhaps you have a question?"
The creature he suggested.
And he flew up and landed on my hand.
But all the things I'd wondered,
I couldn't then remember.
My thoughts, it seemed, had just turned into sand.

So, I asked such formal questions,
as one might ask a stranger.
"What's your name?" and
"Do you live close by?"
The creature tipped his head,
he looked like he was thinking, said
"My name is Zed.
Shall I tell you why?"
I told him, "But of course."
And he flapped his wings a little.
This time they seemed electric Bluey -green.
"My name is Zed, as I'm the last
of the Magic Damsel species.
And I have powers no one else has ever seen."
I looked around about.
And I listened quite intently.
Hoping someone else I knew would just come by.
But all the sound there was,
was the tinkling of the water
and the buzzing of a most insistent fly.
"Well Zed", I said, "I'm Mary,
and I'm very glad to meet you.
Will you show me what your magic powers can do?"
And he asked me if I'd like to go on a little journey.
I said "Only if Anubis can come too."

When Anubis heard his name,
He came back to my side
so he could hear what our new friend would reply.
Zed said "But of course,
there is room indeed, for four.
Now close your eyes and whisper 'Damselfly.'"
So, I closed my eyes and whispered,
holding tight to dear Anubis.
When I opened them
it all seemed so bizarre.
For the grasses were like trees,
and the stream more like a sea,
and the damselfly was bigger than a car!

Jump aboard said Zed,
Where would you like to go?
And at once I knew exactly what I'd love.
"To see the Happy Ghost Choir sing"
I said and clapped my hands.
And at once we were soaring high above.
We rose up through the trees,
seemed to float across the fields.
Anubis, safe between my arms and chest.

And his ears flapped in the wind.
When her turned around, I grinned,
as I thought of all adventures this was best.
After several moments flight
we descended where a light was
shining brightly through the windows of a church.
And a simply charming sound
floated high above the ground
where Zed found us the perfect place to perch.
We were right atop a cross,
which was standing in the nave,
and I could hear the songs
of now and days gone by.
Not *churchy* music,
more from movies, pop and classics.
When I saw the choir, I knew the reason why.
For all who sang with passion
were singers who had died,
and each was still the same age that they'd been.
The songs they all knew well
and had sung whilst still alive
were sung with happiness and love.
It was supreme.

We stayed there for a while.
And the tears ran down my face -
not of sorrow, but of joy, and understanding.
Then Zed said "Time to go."
and we jumped up on his back,
and the next thing I recall
was our soft landing.
We came down by the stream
we had left some while ago?
And I checked my watch,
to see what was the time.
The Damsel fly flew off
And landed on a stem.
And indeed, it was very nearly nine.

About the Author

Whilst living in the Tarn, France, Shuna regularly walked with her dog Slippers, the various 'circuits' around the beautiful grounds of Chateau-Musee du Cayla. The Chateau had been the home of sibling poets Maurice (1810-1839) and Eugenie (1805-1848) de Guerin. It was only when Shuna was reading these stories to some friends, as they sat beneath a tree by the little pond, that one of them told her of the relief carving inside the Chateau-Musee du Cayla, of a boy and a girl sitting beneath the tree with a dog. What a magical coincidence.

Dedication

This book is dedicated to all the wonderful friends made whilst living so happily with my wonderful dog Slippers in the little village of Vieux in the Tarn, L' Occitane, France.

Profits from the sale of this book will go to: People for the Ethical Treatment of Animals PETA UK – An NGO committed to ending abusive treatment of animals in business and society.

Acknowledgements

I would like to thank my illustrator friend, Chris Hahner for the lovely images. Also, Peter Pearson for composing the music for the audio version.

Also by Dameon Gibbs

He has been an avid writer since his days in high school during the late 1990s. He enjoys the creative process of all writing genres, whether it be religious, poetic, science fiction, historical, biographies, or action-adventure.

Found in the Storm

The protagonist, Antonio, is a character whose perilous journey forms the backbone of the story. He is a very complex individual with strengths and flaws. His decision to join the Army with the hope of improving his life, only to face a dishonorable discharge, sets the stage for a series of challenges that test his resilience and determination. The story cleverly explores the complexities of Antonio's life as he navigates the aftermath of his choices.

The plot takes a turn when Antonio accepts an under-the-table job flying a helicopter, reminiscent of his military days. The seemingly straightforward task of transporting a package from point A to point B in rural Minnesota becomes a high-stakes adventure, especially when a deadly winter storm sweeps in. The authors create a palpable sense of tension and suspense as Antonio grapples with the decision to risk his life for what initially appeared to be easy money. Will he be able to successfully navigate the helicopter through the blinding, severe snowstorm? How will he survive being on the brink of death?

The Legend of Sunshadow and the Sword of Fire

Embark on a thrilling space adventure, *The Legend of Sunshadow and the Sword of Fire*, chronicles the quest of Jubei Hattori, known as Sunshadow, a seventeen-year-old ninja, as he works to retrieve a stolen jewel with the power to control elements. His former temple brother, Nightblade, is responsible for the theft and Sunshadow must use his mystical bracers to summon the legendary Sword of Fire in order to confront him. Along the way, he encounters alien species, forms new alliances, and faces off against the menacing Shadow Lord who threatens the entire universe. As secrets and betrayals come to light, Sunshadow's skills are put to the test as he grapples with the true nature of good and evil and fights to save the cosmos from darkness.

Rise of the Phoenix: Act 1

Two Bodies: a Skilled Merc, and a Powerful Terrorist... Finding their connection is the responsibility of CIA Analyst Dante Tucker and Delta Force Operative Sgt. Nicholas "Edge" Pierce. It quickly becomes clear that the murdered terrorist is simply the start of something far larger, a plan that intends to shake the foundation of America. The Heart of Miami is in Ruins... Destroyed by a new weapon, wielded by a mysterious organization. Tucker and Edge are on the hunt for those responsible before the next phase of this plan can be launched. But with each encounter they have to question are they the Hunters or the Hunted? In this game of cat and mouse that extends from the Everglades to the mountains of Oregon and the nation's capital itself, Tucker and Edge will stop at nothing to bring down those who are responsible!